Here's what kids and grown-ups have to say about the Magic Tree House® books:

"Oh, man . . . the Magic Tree House series is really exciting!"
—Christina

"I like the Magic Tree House series. I stay up all night reading them. Even on school nights!"
—Peter

"Jack and Annie have opened a door to a world of literacy that I know will continue throughout the lives of my students."
—Deborah H.

"As a librarian, I have seen many happy young readers coming into the library to check out the next Magic Tree House book in the series."
—Lynne H.

Magic Tree House®

For a list of Magic Tree House® Merlin Missions and other
Magic Tree House® titles, visit MagicTreeHouse.com.

MAGIC TREE HOUSE®

#3 MUMMIES IN THE MORNING

BY MARY POPE OSBORNE
ILLUSTRATED BY SAL MURDOCCA

A STEPPING STONE BOOK™

Random House 🏠 New York

For Patrick Robbins, who loves ancient Egypt

Text copyright © 1993, 2014 by Mary Pope Osborne
Cover art and interior illustrations copyright © 1993, 2014 by Sal Murdocca

Visit us on the Web!
SteppingStonesBooks.com
randomhousekids.com
MagicTreeHouse.com

Educators and librarians, for a variety of teaching tools, visit us at
RHTeachersLibrarians.com

Library of Congress Cataloging-in-Publication Data
Osborne, Mary Pope.
Mummies in the morning / by Mary Pope Osborne ; illustrated by Sal Murdocca.
p. cm.
(The Magic Tree House) A First Stepping Stone book
Summary: Jack and his younger sister take a trip in their tree house back to ancient Egypt, where they help a queen's mummy continue her voyage to the Next Life.
ISBN 978-0-679-82424-4 (trade) — ISBN 978-0-679-92424-1 (lib. bdg.) —
ISBN 978-0-375-89420-6 (ebook)
[1. Time travel—Fiction. 2. Mummies—Fiction. 3. Magic—Fiction. 4. Tree houses—Fiction.]
I. Murdocca, Sal, ill. II. Title. III. Series: Osborne, Mary Pope. Magic tree house series ; #3.
PZ7.081167Mr 1993 [Fic]—dc20 92-50665

Printed in the United States of America

83 82 81 80 79

This book has been officially leveled by using the F&P Text Level Gradient™ Leveling System.

Contents

CHAPTER ONE

MEOW!

"It's still here," said Jack.

"It looks empty," said Annie.

Jack and his seven-year-old sister gazed up at a very tall oak tree. At the top of the tree was a tree house.

Late-morning sunlight lit the woods. It was almost time for lunch.

"Shhh!" said Jack. "What was that noise?"

"What noise?"

"I heard a noise," Jack said. He looked

around. "It sounded like someone coughing."

"I didn't hear anything," said Annie. "Come on. Let's go up." She grabbed the rope ladder and started climbing.

Jack tiptoed over to a clump of bushes. He pushed aside a small branch.

"Hello?" he said. "Anybody there?"

There was no answer.

"Jack! Come on!" Annie called down. "The tree house looks the same as it did yesterday."

Jack still felt that someone was nearby. Could it be the person who'd put all the books in the tree house?

"Ja-ack!" called Annie.

Jack gazed over the top of the bushes.

Was the mysterious M person watching him now? Maybe M wanted the gold medallion back—the one Jack had found on their dinosaur adventure. Maybe M wanted the leather bookmark back—the one from the castle book.

There was an M on the medallion and an M on the bookmark. But what did M stand for?

"Tomorrow I'll bring everything back," Jack said loudly.

A breeze swept through the woods. The leaves rattled.

"Come on!" called Annie.

Jack went back to the big oak tree. He grabbed the rope ladder and climbed up.

When he reached the top, he crawled through a hole in the wooden floor. He tossed down his backpack and pushed his glasses into place.

"Hmmm. Which book is it going to be today?" said Annie. She was looking at the books scattered around the tree house.

Annie picked up the book about castles. Just yesterday, the castle book had taken Jack and Annie back to the time of knights.

"Hey, this isn't wet anymore," she said. She handed the book to Jack.

"You're right!" said Jack, amazed. The book had gotten soaked in a castle moat, but today it looked fine. Jack silently thanked the mysterious knight who had rescued them.

"Watch out!" warned Annie. She waved a dinosaur book in Jack's face.

"Put that away," Jack said nervously. The day before yesterday, the dinosaur book had taken them to the time of dinosaurs. Jack silently thanked the Pteranodon who had saved him from a Tyrannosaurus rex.

Annie put the dinosaur book back with the other books. Then she gasped.

"Wow," she whispered. "Look at *this*." She held up a book about ancient Egypt.

Jack caught his breath. He took the book from her. A green silk bookmark was sticking out from between the pages.

Jack turned to the page with the bookmark. There was a picture of a pyramid.

Going toward the pyramid was a long parade. Four huge cows with horns were pulling a sled. On the sled was a long gold box. Many Egyptians were walking behind the sled. At the end of the parade was a sleek black cat.

"Let's go there," whispered Annie. "Now."

"Wait," said Jack. He wanted to study the book a bit more.

"Pyramids, Jack," said Annie. "You love pyramids."

It was true. Pyramids *were* high on Jack's list of favorite things, after knights and dinosaurs—*plant-eating* dinosaurs, that is.

He didn't have to worry about being eaten by a pyramid.

"Okay," he said. "But hold the Pennsylvania

book. In case we want to come right back here."

Annie found the book with the picture of their hometown in it: Frog Creek, Pennsylvania.

Jack pointed to the pyramid picture in the Egypt book. He cleared his throat and said, "I wish we could go to this place."

"Meow!"

"What was *that*?" Jack looked out the tree house window.

A black cat was sitting on a branch right outside the window. The cat was staring at Jack and Annie.

It was the strangest cat Jack had ever seen. It was very sleek and dark, with bright yellow eyes and a wide gold collar.

"It's the cat in the Egypt book," whispered Annie.

The wind started to blow. The leaves began to shake.

"Here we go!" cried Annie.

The wind whistled louder. The leaves shook harder.

Jack closed his eyes as the tree house started to spin.

It spun faster and faster.

Then everything was still.

Absolutely still.

CHAPTER TWO

OH, MAN. MUMMIES!

"*Meow!*"

Jack and Annie looked out the window.

The tree house was perched on the top of a palm tree. The tree stood with about a dozen other palm trees. They were in a patch of green surrounded by a desert.

"*Meow!*"

Jack and Annie looked down.

The black cat was sitting at the bottom of the tree. The cat's yellow eyes were staring up at Jack and Annie.

"Hi!" Annie shouted.

"Shhh," said Jack. "Someone might hear you."

"In the middle of a desert?" said Annie.

The black cat stood up and began walking around the tree.

"Come back!" Annie called. She leaned out the window to see where the cat was going.

"Oh, wow!" she said. "Look, Jack."

Jack leaned forward and looked down.

The cat was running away from the palm trees toward a giant pyramid in the desert.

A parade was going toward the pyramid. It looked exactly like the parade in the Egypt book.

"It's the picture from the book!" said Jack.

"What are those people doing?" asked Annie.

Jack looked down at the Egypt book. He read the words under the picture:

When a royal person died, a grand funeral procession took place. Family, servants, and other mourners followed the coffin. The coffin was called a sarcophagus. It was pulled on a sled by four oxen.

"It's an Egyptian funeral," said Jack. "The box is called a sar . . . sar . . . sar . . . oh, forget it." He looked out the window again.

The oxen, the sled, the Egyptians, and the black cat were all moving in a slow, dreamy way.

"I'd better make some notes about this," said Jack.

Jack liked to make notes. He reached into his backpack and pulled out his notebook. Jack wrote:

coffin called sarcophagus

"We'd better hurry," said Annie, "if we want to see the mummy."

Annie started down the rope ladder.

Jack looked up from his notebook.

"Mummy?" he said.

"There's probably a mummy in that gold box," Annie called up. "We're in ancient Egypt. Remember?"

Jack loved mummies. He put down his pencil.

"Good-bye, Jack!" called Annie.

"Wait!" Jack called.

"Mummies!" Annie shouted.

"Oh, man," said Jack. "Mummies!"

Jack shoved his notebook and the Egypt book into his pack. Then he started down the ladder.

When Jack got to the ground, he and Annie took off across the sand.

As they ran, a strange thing happened. The closer they got to the parade, the harder it was to see it. Then suddenly it was gone. The strange parade had vanished.

But the great stone pyramid was still there, towering above them.

Panting, Jack looked around.

What had happened? Where were the people? The oxen? The gold box? The cat?

"They're gone," said Annie.

"Where did they go?" said Jack.

"Maybe they were ghosts," said Annie.

"Don't be silly. There's no such thing as ghosts," said Jack. "It must have been a mirage."

14

"A what?"

"Mirage. It happens in the desert all the time," said Jack. "It looks like something's there. But it just turns out to be the sunlight reflecting through heat."

"How could sunlight look like people, a mummy box, and a bunch of cows?" said Annie.

Jack frowned.

"Ghosts," she said.

"No way," said Jack.

"Look!" Annie pointed at the pyramid.

Near the base was the sleek black cat. He was standing alone. He was staring at Jack and Annie.

"*He's* no mirage," said Annie.

The cat started to slink away. He walked along the side of the pyramid and slid around a corner.

"Where's he going?" said Jack.

"Let's find out," said Annie.

They dashed around the corner just in time
to see the cat disappear through a hole in the
pyramid wall.

CHAPTER THREE

IT'S ALIVE!

"Where did he go?" said Jack.

He and Annie peeked through the hole in the wall. They saw a long hallway. Burning torches lit the walls. Dark shadows loomed.

"Let's go in," said Annie.

"Wait," said Jack.

He pulled out the Egypt book and turned to the section on pyramids.

He read the caption aloud:

Pyramids were sometimes called
Houses of the Dead. They were nearly
all solid stone, except for the burial
chambers deep inside.

"Wow. Let's go there. To the burial chambers," said Annie. "I bet a mummy's there."

Jack took a deep breath.

Then he stepped out of the hot, bright sunlight into the cool, dark pyramid.

The hallway was silent.

Floor, ceiling, walls—everything was stone. The floor slanted up from where they stood.

"We have to go farther inside," said Annie.

"Right," said Jack. "But stay close behind me. Don't talk. Don't—"

"Go! Just go!" said Annie. She gave him a little push.

Jack started up the slanting floor of the hallway.

Where was the cat?

The hallway went on and on.

"Wait," said Jack. "I want to look at the book."

He opened the Egypt book again. He held it below a torch on the wall. The book showed a drawing of the inside of the pyramid.

"The burial chamber is in the middle of the pyramid. See?" Jack said. He pointed to the drawing. "It should be straight ahead."

Jack tucked the book under his arm. Then he and Annie headed deeper into the pyramid.

Soon the floor became flat. The air felt different—musty and stale.

Jack opened the book again. "I think we're almost at the burial chamber. See the picture? The hallway slants up. Then it gets flat. Then you come to the chamber. See, look—"

"*Eee-eee!*" A strange cry shot through the pyramid.

Jack dropped the Egypt book.

Out of the shadows flew a white figure.

It swooshed toward them!

A mummy! Jack thought.

"It's alive!" Annie shouted.

CHAPTER FOUR

BACK FROM THE DEAD

Jack pulled Annie down.

The white figure moved swiftly past them, then disappeared into the shadows.

"A mummy," said Annie. "Back from the dead!"

"F-forget it," stammered Jack. "That's impossible." He picked up the Egypt book.

"What's this?" said Annie. She lifted something from the floor. "Look. The mummy dropped this thing."

It was a gold stick about a foot long. A dog's head was carved on one end.

"It looks like a scepter," said Jack.

"What's that?" asked Annie.

"It's a thing kings and queens carry," said Jack. "It means they have power over the people."

"Come back, mummy!" Annie called. "We found your scepter. Come back! We want to help you!"

"Shush!" said Jack. "Are you nuts?"

"But the mummy—"

"That was no mummy," said Jack. "It was a person. A real person."

"What kind of person would be inside a pyramid?" asked Annie.

"I don't know," said Jack. "Maybe the book can help us."

He flipped through the book. At last he found a picture of a person in a pyramid. He read:

Tomb robbers often stole the treasure buried with mummies. False passages were sometimes built to stop the robbers.

Jack closed the book. "Not a mummy," he said. "Just a tomb robber."

"Yikes. A tomb robber?" said Annie.

"Yeah, a robber who steals stuff from tombs," said Jack.

"What if the robber comes back?" said Annie. "We'd better leave."

"Right," said Jack. "But first I want to write something down."

He put the Egypt book into his pack. He pulled out his notebook and pencil.

He started writing in his notebook:

tomb robber

"Jack—" said Annie.

"Just a second," said Jack. He kept writing:

tomb robber tried to steal

"Jack! Look!" said Annie.

Jack felt a *whoosh* of cold air. He looked up. A wave of terror shot through him.

Another figure was moving slowly toward them.

It wasn't a tomb robber. It was a lady. A beautiful Egyptian lady.

The lady wore flowers in her black hair. Her long white dress had many tiny pleats. Her gold jewelry glittered.

"Here, Jack," Annie whispered. "Give her this." She handed him the gold scepter.

The Egyptian lady stopped in front of them.

Jack held out the scepter. His hand was trembling.

He gasped. The scepter passed right through the lady's hand.

She was made of air.

CHAPTER FIVE
THE GHOST-QUEEN

"A ghost," Annie whispered.

Jack could only stare in horror.

The ghost began to speak. She spoke in a hollow, echoing voice.

"I am Hutepi," she said. "Queen of the Nile. Have you come to help me?"

Jack still couldn't speak.

"Yes," said Annie.

"For a thousand years," said the ghost-queen, "I have waited for help."

Jack's heart was pounding so hard he thought he might faint.

"Someone must find my Book of the Dead," she said. "I need it to go on to the Next Life."

"Why do you need the Book of the Dead?" asked Annie. She didn't sound scared at all.

"It will tell me the magic spells I need to get through the Underworld," said the ghost-queen.

"The Underworld?" said Annie.

"Before I journey on to the Next Life, I must pass through the horrors of the Underworld."

"What kinds of horrors?" Annie asked.

"Poisonous snakes," said the ghost-queen. "Lakes of fire. Monsters. Demons."

"Oh." Annie stepped closer to Jack.

"My brother hid the Book of the Dead so tomb robbers would not steal it," said the ghost-queen. "Then he carved this secret

message on the wall, telling me how to find it."
She pointed to the wall.

Jack was still in shock. He couldn't move.

"Where?" Annie asked her. "Here?" She
squinted at the wall. "What do these tiny pictures mean?"

The ghost-queen smiled sadly. "Alas, my
brother forgot my strange problem. I cannot see clearly that which is close to my eyes.
I have not been able to read his message for
thousands of years."

"Oh, that's not strange," said Annie. "Jack
has the same problem. That's why he wears
glasses."

The ghost-queen stared in wonder at Jack.

"Jack, lend her your glasses," said Annie.

Jack took his glasses off his nose. He held them out to the ghost-queen.

She backed away from him. "I cannot wear your glasses, Jack," she said. "As you can see, I am made of air."

"Oh, I forgot," said Annie.

"But perhaps you will describe the hieroglyphs on this wall," said the ghost-queen.

"Hi-ro-who?" said Annie.

"Hieroglyphs!" said Jack, finally finding his voice. "It's the ancient Egyptian way of writing. It's like writing with pictures."

The ghost-queen smiled at him. "Thank you, Jack," she said.

Jack smiled back at her. He put his glasses on. Then he stepped toward the wall and took a good long look.

"Oh, man," he whispered.

CHAPTER SIX

THE WRITING ON THE WALL

Jack and Annie squinted at the pyramid wall.

A series of tiny pictures was carved into the stone.

"There are four pictures here," Jack told the ghost-queen.

"Describe them to me, Jack. One at a time, please," she said.

Jack studied the first picture.

"Okay," he said. "The first one is like this." He made a zigzag in the air with his finger.

"Like stairs?" asked the ghost-queen.

"Yes, stairs!" said Jack. "Just like stairs."

She nodded. *That was easy enough,* Jack thought. He studied the second picture.

"The second one has a long box on the bottom," he said. He drew it in the air.

The ghost-queen looked puzzled.

"With three things on top. Like this," said Annie. She drew squiggly lines in the air.

The ghost-queen still seemed puzzled.

"Like a hat," said Jack.

"Hat?" said the ghost-queen.

"No. More like a boat," said Annie.

"Boat?" said the ghost-queen. She sounded excited. "Boat?"

Jack took another look at the wall.

"Yes. It could be a boat," he said.

The ghost-queen looked very happy. She smiled. "Yes. Of course," she said.

Jack and Annie studied the next picture.

"The third one is like a thing that holds flowers," said Annie.

"Or a thing that holds water," said Jack.

"Like a jug?" asked the ghost-queen.

"Exactly," said Jack.

"Yes. A jug," said Annie.

Jack and Annie studied the last picture.

"And the last one looks like a pole that droops," said Annie.

"Like a curved stick," said Jack. "But one side is shorter than the other."

The ghost-queen looked puzzled again.

"Wait," said Jack. "I'll draw it in my note-book. Big! So you can see it."

Jack put down the scepter and got out his pencil. He drew the hieroglyph.

"A folded cloth," said the ghost-queen.

"Really?" said Jack.

"Yes. That is the hieroglyph for a folded cloth," said the ghost-queen.

"Oh. Okay," said Jack.

He looked at the fourth hieroglyph again.

He still couldn't see the folded cloth. Maybe it was like a towel hanging over a bathroom rod.

"So that's all of them," said Annie. She pointed at each picture. "Stairs. Boat. Jug. Folded cloth."

Jack wrote the words in his notebook.

stairs = ⌐╱▔▏   jug = ⟨⟩

boat = ⌣╲╱▽   cloth = ⟩

"So what does the message mean?" he asked the ghost-queen.

"Come," she said. She held out her hand. "Come to my burial chambers."

And she floated away.

CHAPTER SEVEN

THE SCROLL

Jack put the scepter and his notebook and pencil into his pack. The ghost-queen seemed so kind and gentle. He wasn't afraid of her at all anymore.

Jack and Annie followed her deeper into the pyramid. Finally they came to some stairs.

"The STAIRS!" said Jack and Annie together.

The ghost-queen floated up the stairs.

Jack and Annie followed.

The ghost-queen floated right through a wooden door.

Jack and Annie pushed on the door. It opened slowly. They stepped into a cold, drafty room.

The ghost-queen was nowhere in sight.

Dim torchlight lit the huge room. It had a very high ceiling. On one side was a pile of tables, chairs, and musical instruments.

On the other side of the room was a small wooden boat.

"The BOAT!" said Jack.

"What's it doing inside Queen Hutepi's pyramid?" asked Annie.

"Maybe it's supposed to carry her to the Next Life," said Jack.

Jack and Annie went over to the boat. They looked inside it.

The boat was filled with many things—gold plates, painted cups, jeweled goblets, woven baskets, jewelry with blue stones, and small wooden statues.

"Look!" said Jack. He reached into the boat and lifted out a clay jug.

"The JUG!" said Annie.

Jack looked inside the jug. "Something's in here," he said.

"What is it?" asked Annie.

Jack felt inside the jug. "It feels like a big napkin," he said.

"The FOLDED CLOTH!" said Annie.

Jack reached into the jug and pulled out the folded cloth. It was wrapped around an ancient-looking scroll.

Jack slowly unrolled the scroll. It was covered with wonderful hieroglyphs.

"The Book of the Dead!" whispered Annie. "We found it."

"Oh, man." Jack traced his finger over the scroll. It felt like very old paper.

"Queen Hutepi!" called Annie. "We have it! We found your Book of the Dead!"

Silence. "Queen Hutepi!"

A door on the other side of the chamber creaked open.

"Maybe she's in there," said Annie.

Jack's heart was pounding. Cold air was coming through the open doorway.

"Come on," said Annie.

"Wait—"

"No," said Annie. "She's waited thousands of years for her book. Don't make her wait anymore."

Jack put the ancient scroll into his backpack. Then he and Annie slowly started to cross the drafty room.

They came to the open door. Annie went through first.

"Hurry, Jack!" she said.

Jack stepped into the other room. It was nearly bare, except for a long gold box. The box was open. Its cover was on the floor.

"Queen Hutepi?" called Annie.

Silence.

"We found it," said Annie. "Your Book of the Dead."

There was still no sign of the ghost-queen.

The gold box glowed.

Jack could barely breathe. "Let's leave the scroll on the floor and go," he said.

"No. I think we should leave it in there," said Annie. She pointed to the gold box.

"No," said Jack.

"Don't be afraid," said Annie. "Come on."

Annie took Jack by the arm. They walked together across the room to the glowing gold box.

They stopped in front of the box and peered inside.

CHAPTER EIGHT

THE MUMMY

A real mummy, Jack thought.

Bandages were still wrapped around the mummy's skull, but most of the bandages had fallen away from the face.

It was Hutepi. Queen of the Nile.

Hutepi's mummy wasn't beautiful. It had broken teeth, little wrinkled ears, and a squashed nose. Its flesh had withered. Its eyes were hollow sockets.

The rotting bandages on the mummy's body were coming off. Jack could see bones.

"Oh, gross!" cried Annie. "Let's go!"

"No," said Jack. "It's interesting."

"Forget it!" said Annie. She started out of the room.

"Wait, Annie."

"Come on, Jack. Hurry!" cried Annie. She was standing by the door.

Jack pulled out the Egypt book and flipped to a picture of a mummy. He read aloud:

> **Ancient Egyptians tried to protect the body so it would last forever. First it was dried out with salt.**

"Ugh, stop!" said Annie.

"Listen," said Jack. He kept reading:

> **Next it was covered with oil. Then it was wrapped tightly in bandages. The brain was removed by—**

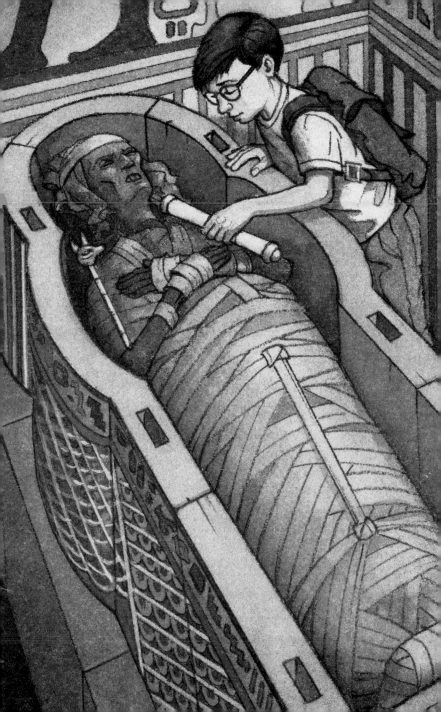

"Yuck! Stop!" cried Annie. "Good-bye!" She dashed out of the room.

"Annie!" called Jack. "We have to give her the Book of the Dead!"

But Annie was gone.

Jack reached into his pack. He pulled out the scroll and the scepter. He put them next to the mummy's skull.

Was it just his imagination? Or did a deep sigh seem to shudder throughout the room? Did the mummy's face grow calmer?

Jack held his breath as he backed out of the mummy room. He hurried through the boat room and headed down the stairs.

At the bottom of the stairs, Jack heaved his own sigh, a sigh of relief.

He looked down the hallway. It was empty.

"Hey! Annie! Where are you?" he said.

No answer.

Where in the world was Annie?

Jack started down the hallway. "Annie!" he called.

Had she run out of the pyramid? Was she already outside?

"Annie!"

"Help, Jack!" came a cry. The voice sounded far away.

It was Annie! Where was she?

"Help, Jack!"

"Annie!"

Jack started to run along the shadowy hallway.

"Help, Jack!" Her cry seemed fainter.

Jack stopped.

He was running *away* from her voice.

"Annie!" he called. He went back toward the burial chambers.

"Jack!" Her voice was louder.

"JACK!"

Jack climbed the stairs. He went back into the boat room. He looked around at the furniture, the musical instruments, and the boat.

Then he saw it. There was another door! It was right next to the door he had just come through!

The other door was open.

Jack dashed through it. He found himself at the top of some stairs.

They were just like the stairs outside the other door.

He went down the stairs and into a hallway. It was lit by torches on the wall.

It was just like the other hallway.

"Annie!" he called.

"Jack!"

"Annie!"

"Jack!" Annie was running through the hallway toward him. She crashed into him.

"I was lost!" she cried.

"I think this is one of those false passages built to fool the tomb robbers," said Jack.

"A false passage?" said Annie, panting.

"Yeah, it looks just like the other hallway," said Jack. "We have to go back into the boat room and out the right door."

Just then they heard a creaking noise.

Jack and Annie turned around. They looked up the stairs.

They watched in horror as the door slowly creaked shut.

A deep sound rumbled in the distance and all the torches went out.

CHAPTER NINE

FOLLOW THE LEADER

It was pitch-dark.

"What happened?" asked Annie.

"I don't know. Something weird," said Jack. "We have to get out of here fast. Push against the door."

"Good idea," said Annie in a small voice.

They felt their way through the darkness to the top of the stairs.

"Don't worry. Everything's going to be okay," said Jack. He was trying to stay calm.

"Of course," said Annie.

They leaned against the wooden door and pushed.

It wouldn't budge.

They pushed harder.

It was no use.

Jack took a deep breath. It was getting harder to breathe and harder to stay calm.

"What can we do?" asked Annie.

"Just . . . just rest a minute," said Jack, panting. His heart was pounding as he tried to see through the darkness.

"Maybe we should start down the hall," Annie said. "Maybe we'll eventually come to . . . to an exit."

Jack wasn't sure about that, but they had no choice.

"Okay, come on," he said. "Feel the wall."

Jack felt the stone wall as he climbed slowly down the stairs. Annie followed.

Jack started down the dark hallway. It was impossible to see anything. But he kept going, taking one step at a time, moving his hands along the wall.

Jack went around a corner. He went around another corner. He came to some stairs. He climbed up. Annie followed.

There was a door. Jack pushed against it. Annie pushed, too. This door wouldn't budge, either. Or was it the same door?

Jack and Annie stopped pushing. It was no use. They were trapped.

Annie took Jack's hand in the dark. She squeezed it.

They stood together at the top of the stairs, listening to the silence.

"*Meow.*"

"Oh, man," Jack whispered.

"He's back!" said Annie.

"*Meow.*"

"Follow him!" cried Jack. "He's going away from us."

Jack and Annie started down the dark hall-way, following the cat's meow. Hands against the wall, they stumbled through the darkness.

"*Meow.*"

Jack and Annie kept following the sound, all the way through the winding hallway.

They went around one corner, then another, and another. . . .

Finally they saw a light at the end of the tunnel. They rushed forward—out into the bright sunlight.

"Yay!" Annie shouted.

But Jack was thinking. "Annie," he said. "How did we get out of the false passage?"

"The cat," said Annie.

"But how could the cat do it?" asked Jack.

"Magic," said Annie.

Jack frowned. "But—"

"Look!" said Annie. She pointed.

The cat was bounding away, over the sand.

"Thank you!" called Annie.

"Thanks!" Jack shouted at the cat.

The cat's black tail waved. Then the cat disappeared in the shimmering waves of heat.

Jack looked toward the palm trees. The magic tree house sat like a bird's nest at the top of one.

"Time to go home," Jack said.

Jack and Annie set off for the palm trees. It was a long, hot walk.

At last Annie grabbed the rope ladder. Jack followed.

Once they were inside the tree house, Jack reached for the book about Pennsylvania.

Suddenly he heard a rumbling sound. It was the same sound he had heard in the pyramid.

"Look!" Annie said, pointing out the window. Jack looked.

A boat was beside the pyramid. It was gliding over the sand like a boat sailing over the sea.

Then the boat faded away into the distance.

Was it just a mirage? Or was the ghost-queen finally on her way to the Next Life?

"Home, Jack," whispered Annie.

Jack opened the Pennsylvania book.

He pointed to the picture of Frog Creek.

"I wish we could go home," he said.

The wind began to blow.

The tree house started to spin.

It spun faster and faster.

Then everything was still.

Absolutely still.

CHAPTER TEN

ANOTHER CLUE

Late-morning sunlight shone through the tree house window. Shadows danced on the walls and ceiling.

Jack took a deep breath. The tree house was back in the Frog Creek woods.

"I wonder what Mom's making for lunch," said Annie. She was looking out the window.

Jack smiled. Lunch. Mom. Home. It all sounded so real, so calm and safe.

"I hope it's peanut butter and jelly sand-wiches," he said.

"Boy, this place is a mess," said Annie. "We'd better make it neater in case M comes back."

Jack had almost forgotten about M.

Will we ever meet M? Jack wondered. *The person who seems to own all the books in the tree house?*

"Let's put the Egypt book on the bottom of the pile," said Annie.

"Good idea," said Jack. He needed a rest before he visited any more ancient tombs.

"Let's put the dinosaur book on top of the Egypt book," said Annie.

"Yeah, good," said Jack. He needed a *long* rest before he visited another Tyrannosaurus rex.

"The castle book can go on the very top of the pile," said Annie.

Jack nodded and smiled. He liked thinking about the knight on the cover of the castle book.

He felt as if the knight was his friend.

"Jack," said Annie. "Look!" She was pointing at the wooden floor.

"What is it?" he asked.

"You have to see for yourself."

Jack walked to Annie and looked at the floor. He didn't see anything.

"Turn your head a little," said Annie. "You have to catch the light just right."

Jack tipped his head to one side. Something was shining on the floor.

He tipped his head a bit more. It came into focus.

It was the letter M! It shimmered in the sunlight.

This absolutely proved the tree house belonged to M. There was no doubt about it.

Jack touched the M with his finger. His skin tingled.

The leaves trembled. The wind picked up.

"Let's go home now," Jack said.

Jack grabbed his backpack. Then he and Annie climbed down the ladder.

As they stood on the ground below the tree house, Jack heard a sound in the bushes.

"Who's there?" he called.

The woods grew still.

"I'm going to bring the medallion back soon," Jack said loudly. "And the bookmark, too. Both of them. Tomorrow!"

"Who are you talking to?" asked Annie.

"I feel like M is nearby," Jack whispered.

Annie's eyes grew wide. "Should we look for M?"

But just then their mother's voice came from the distance. "Ja-ack! An-nie!"

Jack and Annie looked around at the trees. Then they looked at each other.

"Tomorrow," they said together.

They took off, running out of the woods.

They ran down their street.

They ran across their yard.

They ran into their house.

They ran into their kitchen.

They ran right into their mom.

She was making peanut butter and jelly sandwiches.

Here's a special preview of
Magic Tree House® Fact Tracker

Mummies
and Pyramids

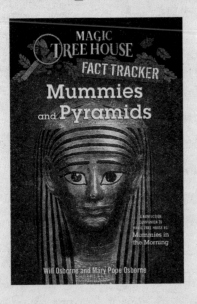

After their adventure in ancient Egypt, Jack
and Annie wanted to know more about mummies
and pyramids. Track the facts with them!

Available now!

Excerpt copyright © 2001 by Will Osborne and Mary Pope Osborne.
Illustrations copyright © 2001 by Sal Murdocca. Published by Random House
Children's Books, a division of Penguin Random House LLC, New York.

Building the Pyramids

It took many years to build a pyramid. It also took thousands of workers.

Egyptologists think the workers used wooden rollers to move giant stones across the desert. Some of these stones weighed over 4,000 pounds!

No one really knows exactly how the workers put the giant stones in place. Most Egyptologists think they built large ramps to raise the stones up the sides of

the pyramid. When the pyramid was finished, the ramps were torn down.

Many people think the work on the pyramids was done by slaves. This is not true. Almost all the work was done by farmers during the flood season.

The farmers were paid to help build the pyramids. But most of them worked for a reason more important than money. They believed building the pyramids would help them get to the Next Life when they died.

Don't miss

Magic Tree House® #4

Pirates Past Noon

Jack and Annie find a secret map
and ruthless pirates. . . .

Available now!

Magic Tree House®

#1: Dinosaurs Before Dark
#2: The Knight at Dawn
#3: Mummies in the Morning
#4: Pirates Past Noon
#5: Night of the Ninjas
#6: Afternoon on the Amazon
#7: Sunset of the Sabertooth
#8: Midnight on the Moon
#9: Dolphins at Daybreak
#10: Ghost Town at Sundown
#11: Lions at Lunchtime
#12: Polar Bears Past Bedtime
#13: Vacation Under the Volcano
#14: Day of the Dragon King
#15: Viking Ships at Sunrise
#16: Hour of the Olympics
#17: Tonight on the *Titanic*
#18: Buffalo Before Breakfast
#19: Tigers at Twilight
#20: Dingoes at Dinnertime
#21: Civil War on Sunday
#22: Revolutionary War on Wednesday
#23: Twister on Tuesday
#24: Earthquake in the Early Morning
#25: Stage Fright on a Summer Night
#26: Good Morning, Gorillas
#27: Thanksgiving on Thursday
#28: High Tide in Hawaii

Magic Tree House®
Merlin Missions

#1: Christmas in Camelot
#2: Haunted Castle on Hallows Eve
#3: Summer of the Sea Serpent
#4: Winter of the Ice Wizard
#5: Carnival at Candlelight
#6: Season of the Sandstorms
#7: Night of the New Magicians
#8: Blizzard of the Blue Moon
#9: Dragon of the Red Dawn
#10: Monday with a Mad Genius
#11: Dark Day in the Deep Sea
#12: Eve of the Emperor Penguin
#13: Moonlight on the Magic Flute
#14: A Good Night for Ghosts
#15: Leprechaun in Late Winter
#16: A Ghost Tale for Christmas Time
#17: A Crazy Day with Cobras
#18: Dogs in the Dead of Night
#19: Abe Lincoln at Last!
#20: A Perfect Time for Pandas
#21: Stallion by Starlight
#22: Hurry Up, Houdini!
#23: High Time for Heroes
#24: Soccer on Sunday
#25: Shadow of the Shark
#26: Balto of the Blue Dawn
#27: Night of the Ninth Dragon

Magic Tree House®
Super Edition

#1: WORLD AT WAR, 1944

Magic Tree House®
Fact Trackers

DINOSAURS

KNIGHTS AND CASTLES

MUMMIES AND PYRAMIDS

PIRATES

RAIN FORESTS

SPACE

TITANIC

TWISTERS AND OTHER TERRIBLE STORMS

DOLPHINS AND SHARKS

ANCIENT GREECE AND THE OLYMPICS

AMERICAN REVOLUTION

SABERTOOTHS AND THE ICE AGE

PILGRIMS

ANCIENT ROME AND POMPEII

TSUNAMIS AND OTHER NATURAL DISASTERS

POLAR BEARS AND THE ARCTIC

SEA MONSTERS

PENGUINS AND ANTARCTICA

LEONARDO DA VINCI

GHOSTS

LEPRECHAUNS AND IRISH FOLKLORE

RAGS AND RICHES: KIDS IN THE TIME OF
   CHARLES DICKENS

SNAKES AND OTHER REPTILES

DOG HEROES

ABRAHAM LINCOLN

PANDAS AND OTHER ENDANGERED SPECIES

HORSE HEROES

HEROES FOR ALL TIMES

SOCCER

NINJAS AND SAMURAI

CHINA: LAND OF THE EMPEROR'S GREAT
   WALL

SHARKS AND OTHER PREDATORS

VIKINGS

DOGSLEDDING AND EXTREME SPORTS

DRAGONS AND MYTHICAL CREATURES

WORLD WAR II

More Magic Tree House®

GAMES AND PUZZLES FROM THE TREE HOUSE

MAGIC TRICKS FROM THE TREE HOUSE

MY MAGIC TREE HOUSE JOURNAL

MAGIC TREE HOUSE SURVIVAL GUIDE

ANIMAL GAMES AND PUZZLES

MAGIC TREE HOUSE INCREDIBLE FACT BOOK

Crabtree Publishing Company
www.crabtreebooks.com

PMB 16A, 350 Fifth Avenue,
Suite 3308,
New York, NY 10118

616 Welland Avenue,
St. Catharines, Ontario
Canada, L2M 5V6

For Katherine, Jack, Andrew and Lauren with love
F.G.E.

Cataloging-in-Publication data is available at the Library of Congress

Published by Crabtree Publishing in 2006
First published in 2002 by Egmont Books Ltd.
Text copyright © Franzeska G. Ewart 2002
Illustrations copyright © Mark Oliver 2002
The author and illustrator have asserted their moral rights.
Paperback ISBN 0-7787-2744-0
Reinforced Hardcover Binding ISBN 0-7787-2722-X

1 2 3 4 5 6 7 8 9 0 Printed in Italy 4 3 2 1 0 9 8 7 6 5

Speak Up, Spike!

Franzeska
G. Ewart

Mark Oliver

Go Bananas

Chapter 1

SPIKE WAS A little boy who lived in a big house, full of big brothers, big sisters, and several huge cousins. His dad was big, and his mom was big. Everyone, including the cat, seemed bigger than Spike. And everyone, except Spike, had enormous voices.

When all the big people crowded around Spike and boomed down at him, it made him feel very tiny. The louder the big people shouted, the quieter Spike spoke, so eventually his voice was as tiny as a mouse's squeak. People were always saying, "Speak up, Spike!" But he couldn't.

Night time was worst. Spike was especially scared in the dark, because the dark was full of huge monsters.

When he was younger, Spike's mom gave him a night-light shaped like a toadstool, with a frog on the top. It glowed comfortingly beside his bed. Spike knew he shouldn't really need a night-light now, but he just couldn't get to sleep without it.

It was all right, usually, if he stayed in bed. But if he had to get up to go to the bathroom, those monsters were waiting for him . . . And there was one particular monster that scared Spike more than anything.

No matter how slowly and
quietly Spike got up, it would
slither out of bed behind him.
Then, it would slide along
the wall, loom up in front
of him, and block the
bedroom door.

When Spike reached for the
doorknob, the monster's terrible
hand would reach for it too, and
as soon as the door was open,
out it dived into the hall.

Then, something even more
awful happened. In the hall
the monster grew to twice the
size! Its great legs bent and
wobbled up the walls, and
it was so tall that its huge
horny head almost reached
the ceiling. By the time Spike
reached the bathroom door, his
heart was pounding. But even then
the monster would not go away.

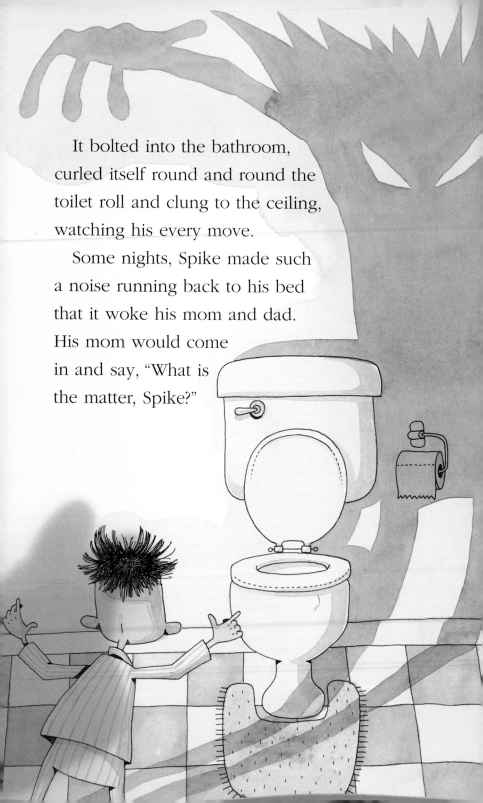

It bolted into the bathroom, curled itself round and round the toilet roll and clung to the ceiling, watching his every move.

Some nights, Spike made such a noise running back to his bed that it woke his mom and dad. His mom would come in and say, "What is the matter, Spike?"

Then Spike would
cuddle into her warm,
comforting nightie and
tell her about the monster.

"Oh Spike!" she would
say, licking her hand and
smoothing his hair down.
"There's no need to be so
frightened, there aren't
really any monsters!"

Sometimes, his dad
came in too.

"Oh Spike!" he would
say, giving him a hearty
pat on his little back.
"You're afraid of your
own shadow! You really
should grow out of it."

When they went away,
Spike would curl into the
smallest ball he could make and bury his head
under the duvet. He wished like anything that
he would grow out of it.

Chapter 2

IT WAS DECEMBER, and the days were frosty and bright. Spike was sitting on the classroom floor with the rest of the class, at Mrs. Pugh's enormous feet.

Mrs. Pugh was the biggest teacher in the world, Spike thought. Even her hair was big. It stood out in huge gray curls, like a lion's mane.

And her voice was so loud you could hear her on the other side of the soccer field, even in a strong gale.

This morning, though, Mrs. Pugh was sitting quietly with her enormous teachers' bag on her knees. She leaned over it and smiled at them all.

"Who knows what the next festival's going to be?" she asked.

Lots of hands shot up. "*Before* Christmas," Mrs. Pugh added, and lots of hands shot down again.

Aftab's hand stayed where it was.

"Divali, Mrs. Pugh," he said.

As soon as the word was out, Spike felt a tiny shiver of delight shoot up the back of his neck. Divali – the Hindu Festival of Lights! He half-closed his eyes and remembered back to last Divali.

They had made divas, little clay pots just big enough to hold a night-light. Spike's had been the biggest, chunkiest diva of all. It had looked a bit like a potato at first, but when he'd drawn a pattern of green triangles and red hearts around it with felt pen, and painted it all over with clear varnish, Mrs. Pugh said, "It's stunning, Spike!"

They had set out all the divas in a long wavy line across the classroom floor, Spike remembered, and they had turned off the lights. Spike hadn't liked that bit at all, but then Mrs. Pugh had crawled along the floor with a box of matches, and she had lit each diva in turn. It had looked beautiful, like a bright, winding snake. The candle smell and the flickering flames had reminded Spike of his own little toadstool night-light at home, and he felt much better.

And when Mrs. Pugh set out four trays of wonderfully sticky Indian sweets called burfee and jalebi, he felt even better.

They all sat looking at the bright little lights, munching their sweets, and singing their Divali song. It was simply wonderful. He was glad it was Divali time again.

"And this Divali is going to be very, very, very special . . ." Mrs. Pugh went on, "because I've brought some very, very, very special people to show you . . ."

She smiled mysteriously and reached inside her big bag. Out came the strangest person Spike had ever seen. He seemed to be covered in spikes himself!

"This," Mrs. Pugh whispered, "is a shadow puppet. His name is Rama."

She held Rama up to the window.

"He's from India, and he's made of leather," she explained. "Later, when we turn off the lights, you'll see his shadow!"

Spike's stomach turned over. All the spit in his mouth dried up, so his tongue stuck to his teeth. And, right at the very backs of his eyes, two big tears began to grow.

A great shadow had been cast over wonderful Divali.

Chapter 3

"DOES ANYONE REMEMBER who Rama is?" Mrs. Pugh asked, waving the spiky shadow puppet above their heads.

Veronica put up her hand and said, "He's the brave prince in the Divali story, Mrs. Pugh."

Mrs. Pugh beamed at Veronica.

"That's right!" she said. "What was the story called?"

"Rama and Sita, Miss," said Aftab, and Mrs. Pugh beamed again.

"Correct!" she smiled.

Mrs. Pugh sat back in her big chair, half-closed her eyes, and, in a very soft and mysterious voice, she told them,

"Long, long, long ago in India, there lived a brave and handsome prince called Rama. He was deeply in love with a princess called Sita."

Mrs. Pugh rummaged around in her bag and brought out another shadow puppet. Everyone went "Ooooooooh!" because Princess Sita was very beautiful.

"I want to be her," Veronica whispered under her breath.

"But the story gets quite sad, doesn't it?" Mrs. Pugh went on. "Because Prince Rama had to go far away, and it was very dangerous. He didn't want Sita to come with him, but she was so deeply in love with him that she did."

Mrs. Pugh closed her eyes. "A woman's place is at the side of the man she loves . . ." she said dreamily.

Aftab put his hand up and snapped his fingers. Mrs. Pugh opened her eyes again.

"The monster came and took Sita away, didn't he, Mrs. Pugh?"

"That's right, Aftab," said Mrs. Pugh. "Prince Rama had gone hunting in the forest, and he told Sita never, ever to step outside the magic circle he had drawn around their house. But the monster, Ravana, came disguised as a deer, didn't he, and tricked poor Sita. She stepped out of the circle, and he changed back and whisked her away to Sri Lanka!"

Spike's mouth got drier and drier as he
watched Mrs. Pugh's hand slip inside the
bag again.

"Can anyone else tell us what Ravana looked
like when he wasn't disguised?" she asked, as
she slowly pulled out another shadow puppet.
It was far bigger than the others.

Gently pushing Aftab's hand back down,
Mrs. Pugh said, "Yes, James, you tell us!"

"He had," James gulped, "ten heads, and he
was vicious."

"*That's* a good word, James," Mrs. Pugh said.
"Vicious is a very good word for Ravana!"

Spike shuddered.

Vicious, he thought, was a very good word.

"Here we are!" smiled Mrs. Pugh, holding the biggest, spikiest shadow puppet up to the light.

Spike covered his eyes with his hands.

"Ravana!" cried Mrs. Pugh. "Who, I am perfectly sure," she added, looking pointedly at Spike, "has a very big voice!"

She leaned over and gave Spike a gentle pat on the head with one of Ravana's hands. Spike opened two of his fingers and gulped.

He peered at Ravana through the slits between his fingers.

Mrs. Pugh climbed carefully over
everyone's heads till she stood at her desk.
There was a wooden picture frame stuck
to the edge of the desk, and Mrs. Pugh
began to stretch a cotton sheet over it.

As she did, she explained,
"Now, for there to be a shadow,
there needs to be light. And
light comes from . . ."

She looked over the picture
frame, and raised her eyebrows,
which meant she was asking
a question.

"Sun!" shouted Aftab.

"Good, Aftab," said Mrs. Pugh. "But today we need a smaller light, so you may pull down the blinds. Where else does light come from?"

"An electric light!" shouted Veronica.

"Splendid," said Mrs. Pugh. "Inside this projector is an electric light! When I turn the projector on, the light will shine on to the screen. But to see it we'll need to turn the classroom lights off!"

Spike watched in horror as she strode over to the light switches, and he gave a little gasp as she flicked them off.

The classroom was plunged into inky darkness. Spike felt his fingernails dig into the skin on the sides of his knees.

"Now, just you wait and see what happens next!" Mrs. Pugh's big voice thundered out above Spike's head.

"Ready?"

There was a soft "click", and the sheet lit up into a bright rectangle of light.

"See?" said Mrs. Pugh. "We've got our own magic little world now."

She disappeared behind the screen and then, suddenly, her great big shadow head filled the whole rectangle, with a jungle of gigantic curls.

"And here comes . . . Ravana!" she announced importantly.

Spike nearly jumped right off the floor as Mrs. Pugh's head was replaced by a terrible shadow monster. It was bigger, and jaggier, and scarier, than anything he had met in the bathroom. It had ten huge heads!

"Ravana's about, so you'd better watch out!" Mrs. Pugh boomed, and everyone clung together and pretended to be terrified.

"And that," she added, popping her head above the screen, "is how *you* are going to have to do it tomorrow. Because *you* are going to act out the Divali story yourselves."

Everyone, except Spike, gasped in delight and said, "Cool!"

"I hope I get to be Rama, the brave prince," said Aftab wistfully.

"I hope I get to be Sita, the beautiful princess," sighed Veronica. "A woman's place is by the side of the man she loves," she added, looking over at Aftab.

Spike said nothing. He was darned sure he wasn't going to *be* anyone.

Chapter 4

SPIKE THOUGHT ABOUT shadows all night
long, especially when he went to the bathroom.
He looked up at the shadow monster, stretching
up behind the toilet, and he felt it looking back
down at him.

He thought about Ravana, the vicious
ten-headed monster, and his hugely scary
shadow. He thought about Mrs. Pugh, tapping
him gently on the head with one of Ravana's
hands. And he remembered how, when Mrs.
Pugh had turned the light back on, Ravana's
shadow had simply vanished!

Actually, when you really saw Ravana, he wasn't that big.

Okay, he had ten heads, but none of them were really all that scary.

He was just a leather puppet, after all. He was even smaller than Spike.

When Spike had flushed the toilet and closed the bathroom door behind him, he tiptoed slowly and quietly back to bed. Then, he lifted the duvet and peered into the darkness. You couldn't see anything, he thought. It was one great big shadow in there.

He curled up in a ball and hugged his knees, and as he did, he wondered whether his shadow was lying beside him hugging its knees too, safe inside their blanket of darkness.

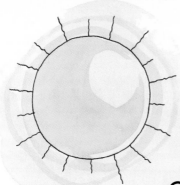

Chapter 5

EARLY NEXT MORNING, Spike was in the playground with a trash bag, picking up litter. Although it was very cold, the sun shone brightly.

Spike collected litter to earn "Sunshine Points", which were special stickers you got if you did a Good Thing. The class with the most "Sunshine Points" got a special "Sunshine Party". It was always a wonderful treat.

The next "Sunshine Party" would be a special Divali one, so there would be mountains of burfee and jalebi, like last year, only far, far, far more.

Grade 3 had never won a "Sunshine Party". They were the only class in the whole school that hadn't, and Spike was sure it made Mrs. Pugh feel really bad.

As he collected, he wondered what was
going to happen today when they did their
Divali shadow puppet play. His stomach
gave a little lurch and his mouth
went dry just thinking about it.

Suddenly, Spike gasped.
There was a monster in
the playground with him.
It had spiky hair, just like
his, and it had its own,
almost-empty trash bag!
It was huge!

Very carefully, Spike lifted one leg so that it stuck right out to the side. The shadow monster stuck its big leg out too. Spike put his leg down again and slowly, wobbling a great deal, he stuck out the other one. It looked really funny. He wiggled his foot around.

The huge shadow foot wiggled too. He kept on doing it, over and over and over again. And then the shadow monster disappeared, drowned in a great black sea. Spike felt a big hand on his shoulder and, looking down, he saw Mrs. Pugh's enormous feet planted one on either side of his own.

"What are you doing, Spike? The bell's long gone!" Mrs. Pugh said angrily.

"I'm playing with my shadow," Spike whispered.

"Speak up, Spike!" Mrs. Pugh shouted.

"I'm playing with my shadow," Spike repeated.
Then he turned around and, in a voice he had
never heard before, he said,

"I don't think I'm scared of my shadow any
more."

"Good!" said Mrs. Pugh, twisting Spike around
and marching him in the direction of the door.
Spike squinted up at her. She had a very funny
look on her face, he thought. She was up to
something.

When they reached the classroom door, Mrs. Pugh stopped and crouched down so that she was level with Spike. Spike blinked several times. He had never been this close to a teacher before.

"Know how many Sunshine Points we need to win the Sunshine Party, Spike?" Mrs. Pugh said.

Spike shook his head.

"Ten," said Mrs. Pugh.

Spike blinked again. Mrs. Pugh's nose was so close he could see his face reflected in her glasses. He did not speak.

"Know how someone could earn us those ten Sunshine Points, Spike?" Mrs. Pugh whispered, and as she did, she winked.

Spike wrinkled his little brow. He bit his lip.

"How, Mrs. Pugh?" he asked.

"You'll see," Mrs. Pugh answered, and pushed him gently through the door.

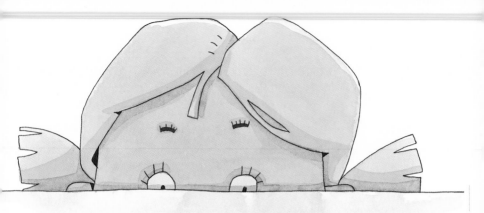

Chapter 6

EVERYONE STARED AT Spike, who sat down
on the floor and tried to look tiny. Veronica was
glaring out from behind the shadow screen,
holding the Sita puppet.

"All right, Veronica and Aftab," said Mrs. Pugh
briskly. "Let's hear your lines again. Then Ravana
will make his entrance."

She turned off the lights and the screen
glowed. There was a great deal of scuffling, and
for a moment all that was seen was the shadow
of Veronica's head. Then Aftab's appeared, and
the two shadows frowned at one another.

"Sit down, for goodness sake!" Mrs. Pugh
growled. "We don't want to see you. We want to
see Rama and Sita!"

At last, the shadowy Veronica and Aftab disappeared, and everyone gasped as Rama and Sita stood before them. The puppets wobbled, and Veronica cleared her throat.

"Oh Rama!" she said, in a very high voice. "Do not leave me! I am so afraid!"

There was silence and both puppets slithered off the screen.

"It's you!" Veronica hissed. "Do not be afraid my darling . . ."

Aftab's head popped out. His face was very red.

"Miss, do I have to call her *my darling?*" he said. "Can I not just call her *Sita*?"

Mrs. Pugh sighed. "You are deeply in love with her, Aftab, like it or not," she said wearily.

As she spoke, she pulled Spike to his feet. Spike felt Ravana's sticks pressed into his hands, and he wobbled under the weight of the big shadow puppet.

"Do not be afraid . . . my darling!" Aftab's voice floated through the darkness. "Stay in the magic circle and you will . . . you will . . ."

"You will come to no harm!" shouted Mrs. Pugh. She steered Spike into the pool of light and pushed him down.

"Come on," she whispered in his ear. "Say, *'Ravana's about, so you'd better watch out!'*"

Spike swallowed hard and stuck the shadow puppet into the overhead projector's beam. Ravana's shadow filled the screen. Spike gazed dizzily up at him. He pulled the puppet towards him so that its shadow grew even bigger.

He had never seen anything so huge. His heart pounded and his tongue stuck to the roof of his mouth.

Mrs. Pugh knelt down beside him. She held one of the sticks for him, and together they made Ravana move out and in. He grew bigger, then smaller, then bigger again.

"Come on, Spike," Mrs. Pugh whispered, giving him a nudge. "There's ten Sunshine Points in it if you do!"

Spike took a deep breath. He thought how pleased Mrs. Pugh would be if they won a Sunshine Party at last. But his mouth was so dry his tongue just wouldn't move.

He thought about great mountains of burfee and jalebi. He thought about pink burfee, and green burfee, and burfee with nuts in . . . Spike licked his lips. Then he looked up at the great big shadow monster in his hands and he shouted, "Ravana's about, so you'd better watch out!"

"Great, but speak up, Spike," whispered Mrs. Pugh gently. "Do it really viciously. *You're* the big monster now!"

This time, when Spike did his lines, it felt like the whole school would come crashing down on top of him.

"RAVANA'S ABOUT," he boomed, "SO YOU'D BETTER WATCH OUT!"

His voice was so loud, and so ferocious, that Veronica stepped backwards into Aftab, and they both landed on the floor in a mass of sticks and leather.

"Well done, Spike!" said Mrs. Pugh. She disentangled Veronica and Aftab from Rama and Sita, dusted them off, and then switched the classroom lights back on.

"A magnificent performance," she beamed, pulling Spike out from behind the screen and holding Ravana high above his head. "And worth ten Sunshine Points, I think!"

Spike crawled back into the crowd of children on the floor. Everyone patted him on the back and told him how scary he'd been.

"You were truly vicious, Spike," said Veronica admiringly.

"You've won us our first Sunshine Party, Spike," Aftab said. "It'll be the best Divali ever!"

But Spike wasn't listening. He was thinking about how big he'd made Ravana's shadow grow.

He was thinking about how scary he had made Ravana be.

And, most of all, he was thinking about the big, deep voice he'd never known he had. It could scare even the biggest monster away!

Spike smiled happily. It was going to be the best Divali ever, without a shadow of a doubt.

Find a flashlight and turn off the light in your room, so it's very dark! Then turn on your flashlight and point it at the wall. What you see is a light beam! Light travels in a straight line, until something gets in its way, like a wall.

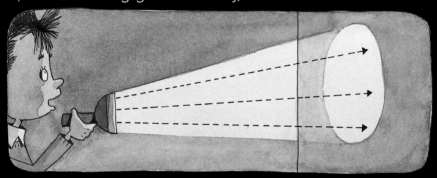

Put your hand over the light, so it covers the beam. What happens?

A thing that blocks light is described as opaque.

Try putting your hand in the light's beam. What happens now?

Some of the light is blocked by my hand and a shadow is formed!

Move your hand around. What does your shadow do?
Look what happens if I move my hand closer to the flashlight.
My shadow gets bigger!

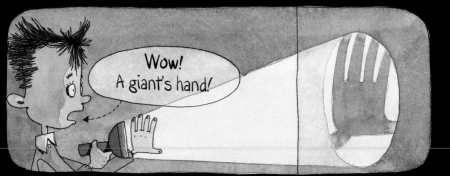

This is because more light is blocked when my hand is
close to the flashlight than when it is further away.

A long time ago, a scientist was climbing
the Brocken Mountain in Germany.
Suddenly, he became aware of a
huge, scary figure in front of him in
the clouds. It was far bigger than the
monster in my bathroom. It was even
bigger than Ravana! But it was only
his shadow!

Just as the flashlight
cast a shadow of my
hand against the wall, the
sun cast a shadow of the
climber on the passing clouds.

What you will need:

- 1 big sheet of black construction paper or cardboard
- 1 pencil or pen
- 1 pair of scissors
- 1 thin dowel or knitting needle
- Some sticky tape
- 1 good, strong flashlight
- 1 space on a light colored wall
- 1 hole puncher
- 1 dark night

Make your own Spooky
Shadow Puppet!

1 Think of a scary figure! Now draw it on your page. Remember it needs to be big! Bigger than this book when it's open. It could look like these:

I'm not scared!

2 Carefully cut out your figure and stick the dowel to the back, like this:

3 You can use the hole puncher to make eyes.

4 Wait until night. Close the curtains, draw the blinds, and turn the lights off!

5 Turn your flashlight on and point it at the wall. A circle of light should appear. What happens if you move your flashlight further away from the wall? That's right, the circle grows! Once the light is the size of a trash can lid or bigger, rest your flashlight on a chair.

6 Now put your puppet in the light beam. See how its shadow grows and shrinks as you move the puppet in and out?

Aaaaagh!

7 Give your monster a voice. What scary things might he say?

Speak up!
I didn't hear you.